Elliot and the Impossible Fish

Story by Rebecca North
Illustrations by Laurel Keating

Tuckamore Books
a Creative Publishers imprint

St. John's, Newfoundland and Labrador, 2017

2017, Rebecca North

We gratefully acknowledge the financial support of the Canada Council for the Arts,
the Government of Canada through the Canada Book Fund (CBF),
and the Government of Newfoundland and Labrador through the Department
of Tourism, Culture and Recreation for our publishing program.

Cover Design by Nancy Keating
Illustrations by Laurel Keating
Printed on acid-free paper

Published by
Tuckamore Books
an imprint of CREATIVE BOOK PUBLISHING
a Transcontinental Inc. associated company
P.O. Box 8660, Stn. A
St. John's, Newfoundland and Labrador A1B 3T7
Printed in Canada

Library and Archives Canada Cataloguing in Publication

North, Rebecca, 1986-, author
Elliot and the impossible fish / Rebecca North ; illustrated
by Laurel Keating

ISBN 978-1-77103-102-8 (softcover)

I. Keating, Laurel, 1990-, illustrator II. Title.

PS8627.O783E44 2017   jC813'.6   C2016-907456-0

For my parents, Barbara and Robert,
who taught me that nothing is impossible.
– Rebecca

For Nan and Pop
– Laurel

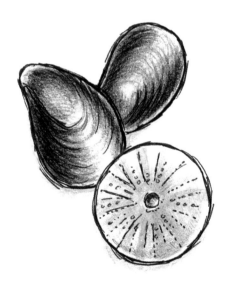

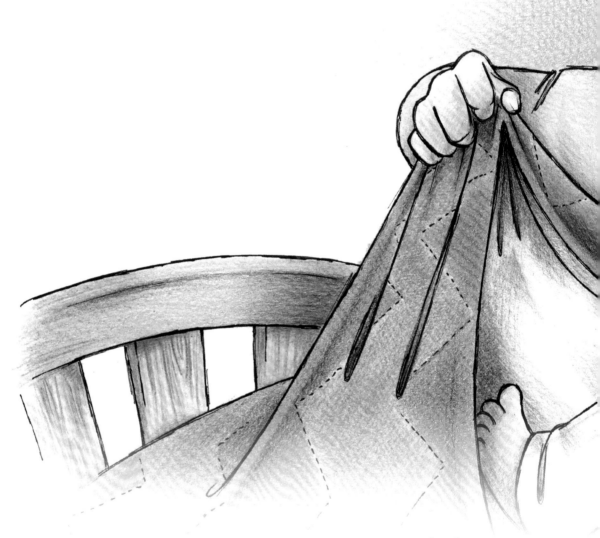

Elliot wanted to catch the biggest fish that anyone had ever seen. He wanted to catch a fish so big it would be on TV.

Elliot's dad was a fisherman. He worked on a big fishing boat out on the ocean. Elliot wanted to be a fisherman too.

One night, as Elliot's dad was tucking him into bed, Elliot asked, "Can I come fishing with you tomorrow?"

"Not tomorrow Elliot, I have to work, but we can go fishing at the lake this weekend."

"No, no, no, I don't want to go fishing on a lake. I want to come to work with you and fish on the ocean. That's where there are GIGANTIC fish."

"No Elliot. You can come when you are older. Right now, you are too little."

"Pllllleeeeease?" asked Elliot.

Elliot's dad shook his head. "Sorry Elliot, it's just not possible." Then he turned out the light and closed the door.

Elliot looked out his bedroom window and saw a very bright star in the sky.

"I wish I could catch the biggest fish that anyone has ever seen," Elliot whispered. Then he closed his eyes and went to sleep.

When Elliot woke up, he was surrounded by water. He was on a boat floating in the ocean.

Elliot knew this was his chance to catch a really big fish. He pulled out his fishing rod, put a worm on the end and cast it into the water.

Then he waited, and waited, and waited...

He waited until he heard a voice grumble, "You'll never catch a fish like that!"

Elliot turned around and saw a puffin. "Well…how do you catch fish?" asked Elliot.

"I use my wings to glide through the water and catch fish in my beak. I catch at least ten at a time!" said the puffin proudly. "Go ahead, stretch out your wings and show me how you glide!"

Elliot stretched out his arms as wide as he could.

"Oh…your wings have no feathers to help you glide. You can't catch fish with those wings. It's impossible," said the puffin.

"Just wait and see," said Elliot.
So they waited, and waited, and waited…
They waited until a voice barked, "That's not how you catch a fish!"

Elliot looked and saw a seal beside him. "Well…how do you catch fish?" asked Elliot.

"I use my strong flippers to dive deep down into the water to catch them! Go ahead, show me how strong your flippers are!"

Elliot sat down and kicked his feet in the air.

"Oh…your flippers are very weak. You can't catch a fish with such weak flippers. It's impossible," barked the seal.

"Just wait and see," said Elliot.
So they waited, and waited, and waited…
They waited until a deep voice bellowed, "You won't catch any fish that way!"

Elliot peered over the side of his boat. There, he saw a humpback whale. "Well…how do you catch fish?" asked Elliot.

"I find a spot where there are lots of fish. Then, I swim through the water and open my mouth very wide to catch them. Go ahead, open your mouth really wide!" said the whale.

Elliot opened his mouth as wide as he could.

"Oh…your mouth is very small! You can't catch fish with such a small mouth. It's impossible," bellowed the whale.

"Just wait and see," said Elliot.
So they waited, and waited, and waited…
They waited for a very long time until a sneaky voice
whispered, "Psssst... you want to know how I catch fish?"

Elliot turned around and saw a jaeger sitting on the edge of his boat. "Yes! How?" asked Elliot.

"I don't…" said the jaeger, "I just steal someone else's. I wait until another bird has caught a fish. Then, I fly in as fast as I can and steal it! Go ahead, show me how fast you can fly!"

Elliot ran and took a giant leap.

"Oh…you don't fly very well or very fast, so there's no way you could steal a fish. It's impossible," said the jaeger.

Elliot cast his line back into the water. "Just wait and...
WHOA!" He felt a HUGE tug at the end of his rod. He pulled
and PULLED and PULLLLLLED!

He reeled and pulled until he could see an enormous fish at the
end of his line.

"I don't believe it! That's the biggest fish I have ever seen!" cried the jaeger.

"That must be the biggest fish that ANYONE has ever seen!" shouted the puffin.

The fish tugged and yanked and heaved as hard as it possibly could.

Elliot tugged and yanked and heaved as hard as he possibly could.

Elliot could feel the fish starting to come out of the water. He kept reeling in more line and pulling as hard as he could! The fish finally soared up into the air! Elliot gave one last giant tug to hoist the fish up into his boat and…

...he fell over backwards.

When he stood up, he had a blanket in his hands, not a fishing pole.

He was standing in a bed, not a boat.

He was staring at his bedroom wall, not the ocean.

Elliot shut his eyes tight and opened them again. "…it was all just a dream?"

Elliot's dad walked into his room. "Elliot, there's chocolate chip pancakes for breakfast and… ELLIOT! What HAPPENED in here? Clean up this mess right now or I'm giving ALL of your pancakes to your sister!" cried his dad, stomping out of the room.

"Huh? What?" mumbled Elliot sleepily. He peered over the edge of the bed. "That's impossible…"